MY MEDICO'S
LOVE STORY

ANJI REDDY BAPATHU

TRUE SIGN
PUBLISHING HOUSE

Published by True Sign Publishing House

Address: G-3, HDB Arcade, Door Sanchar Nagar, Gulmohar,
Near UCO Bank, Bhopal, Madhya Pradesh - 462039
E-mail: truesignbooks@gmail.com
Website: www.truesign.in

My Medico's Love Story

Author: Anji Reddy Bapathu

First Edition: 2025

DEDICATION

I want to dedicate this book to my friend Vasavi who inspired me to not to lose the writer in me and my college friends Akshi, Jerry & Tom, who always listen to my stories whenever I want to share. Finally, I wanted to thank my friend Meghana who supported me in Writing this book.

CONTENTS

ACKNOWLEDGMENTS

Writing this book has been a journey, and I am deeply indebted to the many individuals who have supported me along the way.

First and foremost, I want to express my sincere gratitude to my family. Your unwavering belief in me, your patience during late nights and early mornings, and your constant encouragement have been my bedrock. Thank you for understanding when I needed to retreat into the world of my characters.

To my incredible friends, thank you for being my sounding board, my cheerleaders, and my reality checks. Your insightful feedback and your willingness to listen to my endless ramblings about plot twists and character arcs have been invaluable.

CHAPTER - 1

A SMILE THAT HEALED

The loud noise of metal trays and the quick whispers of students made a harsh sound. This was very different from the soft sounds of leaves and birds Karthik knew from his village. He was like a plant moved to a new place, a village boy now in a busy medical college. It was a world of lots of pressure and information. The noise made him feel anxious, like a constant buzzing in his ears. But there was a safe place, a quiet corner: the college store.

It was a place with dusty books, old shelves, and the nice smell of old paper. Here, among the tall stacks of medical books, Karthik could escape the hard work of his first year. He'd get lost in the pages, the detailed drawings and complicated ideas, a good distraction from the stress of school and friends.

One quiet afternoon, the store was almost empty. The only sound was the soft turning of pages as Karthik tried to understand the blood system. He was deep in the details of tiny blood vessels when a light, unexpected sound broke his focus. Soft, sweet laughter, like gentle bells in the wind, came towards him.

He looked up, his eyes going to where the sound came from. And there she was.

Anamika. Even from far away, she seemed bright. She wore the white coat of a student, but it looked almost magical around her. Her eyes, bright and lively, sparkled as she laughed with her friends. A feeling of warmth, like sudden sunlight, came over Karthik.

But her smile was what really caught him. It was a happy smile, a bright light that filled the room, pushing away the darkness and dust. It was like the sun itself had come inside and landed on her face.

People say love at first sight is not real, just a dream. But in that moment, as Anamika's laughter filled the quiet store, Karthik knew it was real. It wasn't a dream, but a bright, true feeling, shown in the warm, golden colors of Anamika's smile.

Karthik was a quiet person. He loved watching Anamika, but he was too shy to talk to her. He saw how smart she was, how kind she was to everyone, and how strong she seemed. It made him feel amazed.

That night, as he fell asleep, he remembered her laughter. It was like a sweet song in his head. It made him feel calm and happy, like a warm hug. He felt a new, gentle warmth in his chest. He slept well, with a happy smile on his face.

The next morning, the lecture hall, usually a place to study, felt like a stage to him. He sat in the back, his heart beating fast, waiting to hear her voice.

"May I come in, sir?"

Her voice, soft and clear, filled the room. His heart jumped. He looked at the door, and there she was. Anamika. Her eyes looked around the room, and for a moment, their eyes met. It was her, the girl from the store, just as bright as he remembered. Everything around them seemed to slow down.

She walked into the room, moving gracefully and confidently. She made the room feel full of a quiet energy. As the teacher started talking, Karthik couldn't focus. He kept looking at Anamika. He saw her writing notes, looking very serious. Her eyes were bright with curiosity, just like his eyes were bright with admiration. He was more interested in her than the lesson. She had captured his heart with just a smile and her sweet laughter.

The more Karthik saw Anamika, the more he liked her, but the harder it became to talk to her. He felt stuck, his heart fighting between wanting her and being scared. He wanted to be close to her, but he was afraid she would say no, which made him feel unsure of himself.

Days turned into weeks, and he liked her more and more. He watched her from far away, amazed by how smart, kind, and strong she was. In the hard world of medical school, she was like a bright light guiding him.

They saw each other in places like the quiet library, the cold dissection room, and the busy canteen. Each time they met, they looked at each other, which felt like a silent talk and a promise of something more.

It was very hard for Karthik to find the courage to speak. He was good with words when studying, but not when talking about his feelings. His mind, usually good at medical terms, became confused and worried. But he really wanted to tell her how he felt, like a strong wave pushing him.

Months passed in a blur of books, dissections, and lots of coffee, as medical school took up all his time. But Anamika was always there, like a bright light in his life. Every time he looked at her, he liked her more, and it felt like a silent love story. He wanted to tell her, but he was too shy.

He wanted to stop being shy and tell her everything, like a waterfall of feelings. But fear of being rejected kept him from doing it.

He knew he couldn't just watch anymore. He had to stop being shy and go into her bright world. He needed to talk to her, take a chance, and hope she felt the same way he did.

The anatomy lab, a realm of stark, clinical precision, was an unlikely theater for the unfolding drama of a hesitant heart. Its air, thick with the antiseptic tang of formalin, clung to the sterile surfaces, a constant reminder of the human body's intricate, fragile mechanics. The stainless steel tables, gleaming under the harsh fluorescent lights, held the silent promise of scientific discovery, yet for Karthik, they were merely a backdrop to the more pressing matter at hand.

He had found himself drawn to this space, not by the allure of anatomical enlightenment, but by the magnetic pull of Anamika's presence. Fate, it seemed, had a peculiar sense of humor, orchestrating their encounters in the most unexpected of settings. The human body, with its complex network of muscles, nerves, and vessels, lay exposed before them, a microcosm of the tangled emotions that churned within Karthik's own heart.

Anamika, her brow furrowed in concentration, was deeply engrossed in deciphering the intricacies of a muscle diagram. Her focus was unwavering, her dedication evident in the meticulous way she traced the lines and labels. She was a picture of quiet intensity, a beacon of intellectual curiosity in the sterile environment. Karthik, a scalpel clutched in his trembling hand, stood a few feet away, his gaze fixed on her. The sharp, metallic instrument felt foreign in his grasp, a stark contrast to the soft, gentle emotions that swelled within him.

He had rehearsed his approach countless times in his mind, each scenario playing out with varying degrees of success. But now, faced with the reality of her presence, his carefully crafted words seemed to dissolve into a jumbled mess of anxieties. He was poised on the precipice of action, ready to finally voice the feelings that had been simmering within him for months.

Just as he was about to take that crucial step, to bridge the distance that separated them, a burst of boisterous laughter echoed through the lab, shattering the solemn atmosphere. Ria, Anamika's closest confidante, a vivacious girl with an infectious smile, had arrived, her energy radiating like a warm, comforting glow.

"Can you believe this muscle, guys? It's like a tiny maze!" she exclaimed, her voice filled with amusement, as she pointed at the diagram. Her laughter, a melodic cascade of sound, filled the room, dispelling the tension that had hung in the air.

Karthik, despite his nervous anticipation, found himself drawn to Ria's vibrant presence. Her infectious energy was a welcome distraction, a momentary reprieve from the turmoil within him. He seized the opportunity, introducing himself, his voice barely audible above the clatter of surgical instruments.

A flicker of recognition sparked in Anamika's eyes. "You're Karthik, right? The quiet one from the library?" she asked, a hint of amusement softening her features. Her voice, gentle and inviting, eased the tension that had gripped him.

A casual conversation ensued, a discussion about the intricacies of human anatomy. They exchanged observations, shared insights, and even managed a few lighthearted jokes. Karthik, emboldened by Ria's presence, felt a surge of newfound confidence. The weight of his anxieties seemed to lift, replaced by a sense of possibility.

He realized that Ria, with her easygoing nature and genuine warmth, could be his bridge, a conduit to Anamika's world. Perhaps, with her help, he could finally find the courage to express the feelings that had been simmering within him for so long. After all, a heart, as complex and delicate as the one they were studying, deserved a gentle, thoughtful approach. And in this unlikely setting, amidst the anatomical wonders, perhaps his own heart would finally find its voice, its hesitant melody rising above the sterile silence of the lab.

The morning sun, filtering through the library's tall windows, cast long, golden rays across the rows of towering bookshelves. Karthik, accompanied by his steadfast friend Anvesh, had sought refuge in this sanctuary of knowledge, hoping to find a moment of quiet amidst the relentless demands of medical school. They settled at a large oak table, their textbooks spread out before them, the silence a comforting balm to their weary minds.

But the tranquility was soon to be disrupted. As they delved into their studies, Karthik noticed Anamika and Ria approaching, their presence a ripple in the library's otherwise serene atmosphere. The library, usually a haven of hushed whispers and rustling pages, was about to experience a shift in its carefully maintained equilibrium.

Ria, with her characteristic burst of energy, immediately transformed their corner of the library into a vibrant hub of activity. She and Anvesh were soon huddled over a particularly daunting anatomical diagram, a labyrinth of lines and labels that seemed designed to confound the most dedicated student. The air, thick with the scent of aged paper and the unspoken tension of academic pressure, crackled with Ria's frustration.

"I swear, this diagram is trying to tell me a secret code!" she exclaimed, her voice rising in exasperation. She squinted at the page, her eyebrows drawn together in a furrow of concentration. "It's like the artist had a personal vendetta against first-year med students."

Anvesh, observing her animated struggle, couldn't suppress a chuckle. "Maybe it's a test of our patience," he suggested, attempting to inject a dose of levity into the situation.

Ria's eyes widened in mock horror. "Oh no, you're right! They're training us to become medical detectives. Next thing you know, we'll be solving murders with our anatomy knowledge."

Their laughter, spontaneous and genuine, erupted, momentarily shattering the library's solemn silence. The tension that had permeated the air dissipated, replaced by a sense of camaraderie. Anvesh, initially reserved, found himself unexpectedly charmed by Ria's infectious energy. She was like a breath of fresh air, a vibrant spark in the otherwise staid environment. As their laughter subsided, a comfortable silence settled between them, a silent acknowledgment of the unexpected connection that had formed. Anvesh realized that he genuinely enjoyed her company.

Karthik, meanwhile, watched the interaction with a quiet sense of hope. He believed that, with Ria's help, he might finally find the courage to express his feelings for Anamika. He, ever the silent observer, tried to focus on his book, but the lively exchange between his friends proved to be a formidable distraction. Anamika, though attempting to maintain a semblance of composure, couldn't suppress a small, amused smile that played at the corners of her lips.

"Guys, can we please try to be quiet?" she pleaded, her voice barely audible above the rising din.

"Sorry, Your Highness," Anvesh replied, bowing dramatically. "We shall endeavor to be as silent as a mouse... after we finish laughing at this ridiculous diagram."

Ria and Karthik joined in the renewed burst of laughter, their attempts to suppress their mirth proving utterly futile. The once serene library, a bastion of quiet study, had transformed into a battlefield of giggles and muffled snorts.

The librarian, with a mask of disapproval, cast a stern glare in their direction. They quickly attempted to regain their composure, but the damage was done. The library, for that brief, chaotic moment, had become a haven for absurdity, courtesy of four medical students with a penchant for laughter and a disregard for the rules of quiet study.

CHAPTER - 2

ANVESH & RIA

Anvesh, Karthik's loyal and slightly chaotic best friend, had always been the life of the party. With his quick wit and infectious laughter, he was the one who could lighten even the darkest moods. But beneath the jovial exterior, there was a sensitive and caring soul.

Ria, with her vibrant personality, was the perfect match for Anvesh's chaotic energy. Their friendship blossomed into something more when they found themselves paired up for a group project. The long hours of studying together turned into shared laughter, inside jokes, and a growing understanding of each other.

Anvesh was drawn to Ria's intelligence and her ability to find humor in any situation. Ria, in turn, appreciated Anvesh's unwavering support and his ability to make her laugh even on the toughest days. Their connection was undeniable, a spark ignited amidst the chaos of medical school.

While Karthik was navigating the complexities of his feelings for Anamika, Anvesh and Ria were quietly building a foundation for their own love story. Their journey was filled with shared dreams, inside jokes, and a deep-rooted friendship that was slowly evolving into something more.

As the days turned into weeks, the camaraderie between Anvesh and Ria deepened. Their shared laughter, inside jokes, and late-night study sessions created an undeniable bond. Anvesh was drawn to Ria's intelligence and her ability to find humor in any situation, while Ria appreciated Anvesh's unwavering support and his infectious enthusiasm.

One evening, after a particularly grueling dissection session, they found themselves alone in the library. The soft glow of the lamps cast long shadows, creating an intimate atmosphere. As they discussed a complex anatomical concept, their eyes met for a moment longer than usual. An electric current seemed to pass between them, a silent acknowledgment of the growing attraction. Anvesh, ever the impulsive one, broke the silence. "You know, I've been thinking," he began, his voice laced with a nervous undertone. "We've been through a lot together. We've laughed, we've cried, we've pulled all-nighters...I think there's something more between us than just friendship."

Ria's heart pounded in her chest. She had been waiting for these words, yet at the same time, she was caught off guard. She looked at Anvesh, her eyes filled with a mixture of surprise and anticipation. "I think so too," she replied softly.

In that moment, under the soft glow of the library lamps, their friendship took a significant step forward. As their hands brushed against each other, a spark ignited, promising a love story that was just beginning to unfold.

With each passing day, their feelings for each other deepened. They spent countless hours together, exploring the city, sharing secrets, and building a life together. Their love story was a beautiful tapestry, woven with threads of laughter, support, and shared dreams.

As they navigated the challenges of medical school, their love for each other became their anchor. They were each other's confidantes, cheerleaders, and partners in crime. Their relationship was a testament to the fact that love could flourish even in the most demanding of circumstances.

CHAPTER - 3

SUMMER BREAK

Summer stretched out before Karthik like an endless, arid expanse. The vibrant chaos of medical school had been replaced by a quiet, almost oppressive stillness. The library, once a bustling hub of activity, now echoed with an eerie emptiness. Without Anamika's laughter, the familiar corners of their shared world felt alien. Days bled into nights, each one a monotonous repetition of the last. He found himself aimlessly wandering through the city, searching for a semblance of normalcy. But the city, once a source of inspiration, now seemed indifferent to his solitude.

The absence of Anamika was a gaping wound, raw and painful. Every shared memory, every inside joke, was a sharp pang of longing. Her laughter, once a melody that filled his days, was replaced by an aching silence. He missed her touch, the warmth of her hand in his, the comforting cadence of her voice.

The world seemed to have lost its color. The food tasted bland, music lacked its usual rhythm, and even the once-enjoyable company of friends felt hollow. His mind was a constant loop of thoughts about her – her smile, her intelligence, her unwavering support.

Nights were the worst. The silence in his apartment was deafening. Without Anamika to share dreams and fears, sleep was elusive. He would lie awake, staring at the ceiling, counting the endless hours until morning.

In the quiet of his solitude, Karthik realized how deeply intertwined their lives had become. She was the missing piece to his puzzle, the melody to his heart. The summer, meant to be a time of relaxation and rejuvenation, had transformed into a relentless test of endurance. With each passing day, his longing for Anamika grew stronger, an insatiable hunger that consumed him.

The weight of loneliness pressed down on Karthik like a physical burden. Every familiar place was now a stark reminder of Anamika's absence. Their favorite café, once filled with shared laughter and inside jokes, was now a desolate expanse. The library, once a sanctuary of shared intellectual pursuits, was now a tomb of solitude.

He found himself drawn to their old haunts, as if by visiting these places, he could somehow feel closer to her. He would sit in their usual corner at the café, drinking a cup of coffee, lost in memories. He would wander through the library aisles, tracing the paths they had walked together, hoping to catch a glimpse of her in the shadows of his imagination.

Nights were the cruelest. The silence of his apartment was a stark contrast to the symphony of their lives together. He missed her laughter, the sound of her typing on her laptop, the gentle rustle of pages as she read. The bed, once a haven of warmth and intimacy, was now a cold, empty expanse.

In the quiet of the night, Karthik would often find himself talking to her, as if she were sitting beside him. He would tell her about his day, his fears, his hopes. He

would laugh and cry, sharing his deepest emotions with the empty air.

The longing for her presence was a constant ache, a gnawing emptiness that refused to be filled. He realized how much she meant to him, how deeply she was woven into the fabric of his life. The summer, meant to be a time of relaxation, had become a painful journey of self-discovery, a stark realization of his dependence on her love.

As the summer wore on, a sense of desperation began to creep into Karthik's solitude. He found himself engaging in impulsive actions, seeking distractions that promised temporary relief. He immersed himself in work, taking on extra shifts at the hospital, hoping to fill the void with exhaustion. But the moment he was alone, the ache in his heart returned, magnified by the silence.

He reached out to friends, seeking solace in their company. While their support was genuine, their presence couldn't replace Anamika's. Their laughter felt forced, their conversations shallow. He felt like a ghost, haunting the margins of their lives.

Desperation pushed him to reach out to Anamika. He drafted countless messages, deleted them, and started again. Words seemed inadequate to convey the depth of his longing, the fear of losing her. He was afraid of rejection, of pushing her away. In the end, he sent a simple text: "I miss you."

Days passed without a response. The silence was deafening. Hope, a fragile ember, flickered and died. Disappointment washed over him, a cold wave of despair. He was alone, truly alone.

Days turned into weeks, and still, no response from Anamika. The initial wave of despair had subsided, replaced by a dull ache of longing. He had resigned himself to the reality of her absence, trying to find solace in the mundane rhythm of his days.

Then, one evening, as he was scrolling through his phone, a notification popped up. A message from Anamika. His heart pounded in his chest as he opened it. "Hey Karthik, I'm so sorry for not replying earlier. I'm currently in Kerala, enjoying some much-needed time with my family. The greenery here is breathtaking, and I've been completely disconnected from the world. Don't worry, I miss you too. I'll be back soon. Can't wait to catch up!"

A surge of relief washed over him. She was alive, well, and missed him. The weight of his loneliness seemed to lift slightly. Yet, a pang of disappointment also crept in. He had longed for her words, her voice, her presence. A simple text, while reassuring, couldn't fill the void that had grown within him.

He replied with a simple smile, "Looking forward to seeing you."

As he put his phone down, he realized that the wait was far from over. The anticipation of her return was both a source of joy and a fresh wave of anxiety. The summer, once a desolate expanse, now held the promise of a reunion. But until then, he would have to find a way to navigate the days, one hour at a time. Summer, with its relentless march of time, finally yielded to autumn. The campus was once again alive with the familiar rhythm of academic pursuits. For Karthik, however, the return to normalcy brought with it a renewed sense of longing. The empty corridors echoed with the absence of Anamika's laughter, her presence a phantom haunting the familiar spaces.

A week passed, and there was still no sign of her. The initial excitement of returning to college had waned, replaced by a growing unease. With each passing day, his hope dwindled, replaced by a creeping fear. He missed her more than words could say the ache in his heart a constant companion.

Impatience, a stranger to Karthik's nature, gnawed at him. He couldn't bear the uncertainty any longer. The fear of losing her, a distant specter, had materialized into a tangible threat. With trembling fingers, he typed a message:

"Anamika, I don't know how to say this, but I can't wait any longer. I love you. I need you here. Please come back soon."

He hesitated, his thumb hovering over the send button. But words had to be said. He hit send, his heart pounding in his chest.

His heart pounded in his chest as he waited for a response. Minutes felt like hours. Finally, his phone buzzed. With trembling fingers, he unlocked it.

Anamika's message read, "I'm back in town. Can we meet at the college canteen tomorrow after college? I need to talk to you."

Relief washed over him, mixed with a surge of excitement. She was coming back. They were going to see each other. But the underlying tension remained. What did she want to talk about? The question hung in the air, a silent specter.

As the day progressed, Karthik found it difficult to concentrate. His mind was

racing, a whirlwind of emotions. He wanted to tell her everything, pour his heart out. But the words seemed inadequate. He needed something tangible, something that could convey the depth of his feelings.

The idea of writing a love letter began to form in his mind. It would be a chance to express himself without the fear of stumbling over his words. He could pour his heart out onto paper, crafting the perfect expression of his love. The thought of handing her a carefully written letter filled him with a sense of anticipation and nervousness.

The night was a restless one for Karthik. He spent countless hours crafting the perfect love letter. Every word was weighed carefully, every sentence a testament to his feelings. By dawn, the letter was complete, a tangible expression of his heart.

The next morning, as he walked into the pathology class, his heart pounded in his chest. The familiar scent of formalin and the sterile environment seemed to amplify his nervousness. Anamika was sitting in her usual seat, her serene demeanor a stark contrast to the turmoil within him.

The lecture felt like an eternity. Karthik's mind was elsewhere, replaying the upcoming meeting with Anamika. He imagined her reaction to the letter, her touch as she read his words. The anticipation was almost unbearable.

The final bell rang, signaling the end of the class. Students began to file out, their voices a distant murmur. Karthik gathered his belongings, his heart pounding in

his chest. He took a deep breath, his eyes locking Anamika's eyes. She nodded, a silent affirmation of their plan. The weight of the letter pressed against his chest as Karthik waited for Anamika outside the college canteen. The autumn sun cast long shadows, and a cool breeze carried the scent of fallen leaves. His heart raced with a mix of anticipation and fear.

Anamika emerged from the canteen; her face framed by the golden hues of the setting sun. She looked tired, but her eyes held a spark of curiosity. They found a quiet corner, away from the prying eyes of other students.

Karthik handed her the letter, his fingers trembling slightly. "I wrote this," he said, his voice barely a whisper.

Anamika took the letter, her fingers tracing the envelope. She looked at him, her eyes filled with questions. Without a word, she opened the letter and began to read.

As she read, Karthik's heart pounded in his chest. He watched her face, searching for any sign of her reaction. Her expression was unreadable, a mask of composure. Minutes felt like hours as she absorbed the words, he had poured his heart into.

As Anamika finished reading the letter, Karthik's heart was in his throat. Her face was a mask of emotions, a storm brewing beneath the surface. He searched her eyes for any clue, any sign of her feelings.

Finally, she looked up, her eyes locked with his. "Karthik," she began, her voice barely a whisper. Her eyes were glistening, a mixture of emotions swirling within them.

Before she could continue, Karthik interrupted, his voice filled with urgency. "Anamika, I know this is sudden, and I know I should have said this in a more romantic setting, but I can't wait any longer. I thought I could die waiting for you to come back into my life. You are my everything.

CHAPTER - 4

I AGREE BUT
I HAVE CONDITIONS

"Karthik, I feel the same way about you. But before you say anything, I have three conditions."

Karthik's heart sank. He had been so caught up in the moment, the possibility of her rejection hadn't crossed his mind. He nodded, his voice barely audible, "I'll listen to anything."

"First," Anamika began, her voice steady, "our relationship exists only within the confines of our MBBS. No promises, no expectations beyond these four years." Karthik's mind raced. It was a harsh condition, but he loved her. He would do anything to be with her, even if it was on her terms. He nodded slowly. "Second," Anamika continued, "you must consider this relationship temporary. No commitments, no future plans. We live in the moment, and that's it." Another blow to his heart. He wanted a future with her, a life built together. But he loved her. He would sacrifice his dreams if it meant being with her, even for a short while. He nodded again.

"And third," Anamika concluded, her voice barely above a whisper, "after our studies, we don't contact each other. No calls, no messages, no attempts to reconnect. It's a clean break."

The world seemed to stop turning. His heart shattered into a million pieces. He had loved her with everything he had, and now, she was asking him to let her go.

But her eyes, filled with a determination that matched the pain in his heart, left him no choice.

He nodded, his voice a mere husk. "I agree."

A cold dread settled over Karthik. He had expected her rejection, but not with such stark, uncompromising conditions. His heart ached with the weight of his love, now laid bare and exposed. Yet, there was a strange sense of clarity during the pain. She loved him, he knew that. But her fear, her insecurities, had created these impenetrable walls.

Anamika's gaze was unwavering, her expression a mixture of determination and sorrow. It was a silent battleground, their hearts locked in a silent war. He wanted to argue, to plead, to convince her of his love. But the words caught in his throat. He nodded, his voice barely a whisper. "I understand."

A heavy silence descended upon them. The world seemed to hold its breath, waiting for the next move. Karthik felt a cold emptiness spreading through him. It was as if a part of him was dying. Yet, he stood tall, his pride a fragile shield against the onslaught of despair.

They sat there for a long time, the weight of their decision hanging heavy in the air. The once vibrant canteen seemed to have lost its color, mirroring the bleakness in their hearts.

A heavy silence descended upon them. The once familiar canteen seemed to shrink, enclosing them in a suffocating bubble. Karthik felt a cold emptiness spreading through him. It was as if a part of him was dying. Yet, he stood tall, his pride a fragile shield against the onslaught of despair.

Anamika looked away; her eyes distant. The weight of their decision seemed to be crushing her too. There was a flicker of pain in her eyes, a silent acknowledgement of the sacrifice they were making.

Minutes turned into what felt like hours. Neither of them spoke, the unspoken words hanging heavy in the air. It was a silent war, a battle of hearts and minds. Finally, Anamika stood up, her voice barely a whisper. "We should get back to class." Her words were a stark contrast to the turmoil within her.

Karthik nodded, his throat dry. He watched as she turned and walked away, her figure a solitary silhouette against the backdrop of the bustling canteen. His heart ached with a pain he had never known before. He was left alone, the weight of their decision pressing down on him like an invisible hand.

The weight of their decision hung heavy in the air, a tangible presence in the once bustling canteen. Karthik watched as Anamika walked away, her silhouette a stark contrast against the vibrant backdrop. The world seemed to have muted its colors, echoing the emptiness within him.

He remained seated, the letter clutched tightly in his hand, a physical manifestation of their broken promise. The future, once filled with hopes and dreams, now stretched out before him, a desolate expanse. The weight of their decision pressed down on him, a crushing burden.

The familiar faces of classmates blurred at the edges of his vision. Their laughter, once a source of comfort, now seemed like a mocking echo. He was a solitary island in a sea of normalcy, his heart adrift in a tempest of emotions.

The days that followed were a blur. The once vibrant campus seemed devoid of life, a sterile backdrop to his internal turmoil. Lectures were a distant echo, their content irrelevant to the storm raging within him. He spent countless hours alone, replaying the conversation with Anamika, searching for answers in the fragments of their exchange.

The love letter, a physical testament to his feelings, lay untouched on his desk, a constant reminder of what could have been. It was a relic of a past that was no longer a haunting echo of a love that was now a prisoner of their own making.

The weight of their decision had become an unbearable burden. Karthik found himself retreating into a shell, his once vibrant spirit subdued by the weight of his loss. The familiar confines of his room, once a sanctuary, had become a prison of memories.

In a desperate attempt to escape the haunting echoes of his past, Karthik decided to move out. A small apartment, located outside the campus, became his new refuge. It was a cold, sterile space, a stark contrast to the warmth and comfort of his previous home.

The act of moving was a physical manifestation of his emotional upheaval. Each item he packed was a reminder of a shared life, a bittersweet memento of their time together. The process was excruciating, a constant reminder of the void that Anamika's absence had created.

The new apartment was devoid of any personal touches. It was a blank canvas, a reflection of the emptiness within him. The walls seemed to close in, amplifying the silence that had become his constant companion. Sleep was elusive, the quiet of the night a stark contrast to the noisy chaos of his mind.

In the solitude of his new home, Karthik was forced to confront his feelings head- on. The initial shock of their decision had begun to subside, replaced by a deep- seated sorrow. He missed Anamika more than ever, her laughter, her touch, the warmth of her presence.

Despite the ache in his heart, Karthik clung to a sliver of hope. Perhaps, he thought, their arrangement was a temporary measure, a test of their love. Maybe, given time, Anamika would soften, her resolve weakening.

Driven by this fragile hope, he invited her to his new apartment. It was a desperate gamble, a last-ditch attempt to rekindle the spark between them. He had decorated the small space, adding personal touches, hoping to create an atmosphere of intimacy. It was a feeble attempt to rewrite their story, to craft a reality where their love defied their own rules.

As he waited for Anamika, his heart pounded in his chest. A mix of anticipation and dread consumed him. He was terrified of rejection, of seeing the harsh reality of their situation reflected in her eyes. Yet, hope, that flickering ember, kept him going.

CHAPTER - 5

CELEBRATION OF LOVE

Anamika arrived on time, her face a mask of composure. Karthik's heart pounded in his chest as he opened the door. The apartment, bathed in soft lamplight, was a stark contrast to the cold, sterile environment he had initially created. He had spent hours arranging it, hoping to create an atmosphere of intimacy.

Anamika stepped inside, her eyes scanning the room. A flicker of surprise crossed her face, but she quickly masked it. "It's cozy," she said, her voice barely a whisper.

Karthik forced a smile. "I wanted to make it feel like home."

A heavy silence settled between them. The carefully crafted ambiance seemed to amplify the tension in the air. Karthik felt a surge of hope, a flicker of defiance against their agreed terms. Perhaps, he thought, tonight could be different.

They sat on the couch, a physical distance mirroring the emotional chasm between them. Karthik reached for her hand, a silent plea for connection. Anamika hesitated, then withdrew her hand. The rejection was a cold slap to his face. The carefully constructed illusion of intimacy shattered like glass. Anamika's withdrawal was a stark reminder of their reality, a sobering counterpoint to his hopeful fantasy.

A heavy silence descended upon them, the only sound the ticking of the clock, a relentless metronome of their shared despair. Karthik felt a surge of anger, a desperate attempt to break free from the icy grip of their situation.

"Why?" he managed to croak out, his voice barely audible. The question hung in the air, a silent accusation.

Anamika looked at him, her eyes filled with a mixture of sadness and determination. "I thought this might change things," she said softly, her voice barely a whisper. "But it hasn't."

Her words were a dagger to his heart. He had hoped against hope that love would conquer all, that their feelings would override their carefully constructed boundaries. But reality had intervened, a harsh and unforgiving mistress.

Anamika, sensing the growing tension, attempted to shift the conversation. "So, tell me about your family," she began, her voice a strained attempt at normalcy. "What do your parents do?"

The question hung in the air, a cruel irony. Karthik was an orphan, a fact he had carefully concealed. His heart clenched as he forced a smile. "My parents... they're not around," he managed to say, his voice barely a whisper.

Anamika's face flushed with embarrassment. "I'm so sorry," she stammered, her eyes filled with remorse. "I didn't know."

Karthik forced a laugh, a hollow sound in the quiet room. "It's okay," he said, his voice trembling slightly. "It's in the past."

But the past was very much present, a ghost haunting the corners of his mind. The silence that followed was heavy, a tangible presence in the room. The attempt at casual conversation had failed miserably, exposing the raw wounds beneath the

surface.

Karthik forced a smile, a bitter taste lingering in his mouth. "It's a long story," he began, his voice barely audible. "I grew up in an orphanage. My parents... they weren't around."

The words hung heavy in the air, a stark contrast to the carefully constructed facade he had maintained. Anamika's eyes widened in shock and sympathy. "I'm so sorry," she whispered, her voice filled with genuine remorse.

A bitter laugh escaped Karthik's lips. "It's okay. It made me who I am today." He paused; his gaze distant. "I wanted to be a doctor, to help people who didn't have the same opportunities I had. To give back, you know?"

Anamika nodded; her eyes filled with a newfound respect. "That's admirable," she said softly.

A fragile silence settled between them, a stark contrast to the emotional turmoil they were both experiencing. In the shared vulnerability of their confessions, a tentative connection began to form. It was a fragile bond, built on shared pain and understanding.

Anamika's eyes welled up with tears. The raw emotion in Karthik's voice had pierced through her defenses. She squeezed his hand, a silent acknowledgment of his pain.

A heavy silence descended upon them, the only sound the ticking of the clock, a relentless reminder of the passage of time. The room seemed to shrink around them, the intimacy they had shared a fragile bubble in a world of chaos.

Finally, Anamika stood up, her voice trembling. "I need some air," she said, her eyes avoiding his gaze.

Karthik nodded, understanding the silent plea. He watched as she turned and walked towards the door, her figure a solitary silhouette against the fading daylight.

He was left alone, the echo of her words hanging in the air. The fragile connection they had forged seemed to be unraveling, pulled apart by the undercurrents of their complex relationship.

The weight of the unspoken words hung heavy in the air. Karthik watched as Anamika retreated into herself, her vulnerability replaced by a protective shell. He wanted to reach out, to offer comfort, but the words caught in his throat.

The apartment, once filled with hope, now seemed like a tomb of their shattered dreams. The ticking of the clock was a relentless reminder of the passage of time, each second a stark contrast to the stillness between them.

A sense of despair washed over him. He had lost her, not just physically, but emotionally. The love they shared, once a beacon of hope, was now a distant memory, replaced by a cold reality. In the quiet of the moment, he realized the depth of his loss. It was more than just the absence of her physical presence; it was the loss of a shared dream, a future they had once imagined together. The pain was a constant companion, a relentless reminder of their shattered hopes.

CHAPTER - 6

EVENING IN THE PARK

The following day, as the sun began its descent, casting long shadows over the city, there was a knock at Karthik's door. His heart pounded in his chest. It was Anamika.

She stood at the threshold, her face etched with a mixture of determination and

vulnerability. "Can we talk?" Her voice was barely a whisper.

Karthik nodded, unable to form words. He stepped aside, allowing her to enter. The familiar scent of her perfume filled the room, a bittersweet reminder of their shared past.

"I need to get out of here," she said, her voice trembling. "Let's go to the park." Without waiting for a response, she turned and walked towards the door. Karthik hesitated for a moment, his mind a whirlwind of conflicting emotions. Then, with a heavy heart, he followed her.

The park was a world away from the sterile confines of their apartments. The soft glow of the setting sun cast long shadows over the manicured lawns, creating an ethereal atmosphere. Anamika and Karthik found a secluded bench, the gentle rustling of leaves providing a soothing backdrop to their silent conversation.

Anamika was the first to break the silence. "I'm sorry," she began, her voice barely audible. "I know I hurt you."

Karthik nodded his throat tight. The words he wanted to say seemed to have vanished, replaced by heavy silence.

Anamika, sensing Karthik's despair, decided to take a different approach. "Remember that time we tried to build a sandcastle and it got washed away by a wave?" she asked, a mischievous glint in her eye.

Karthik managed a weak smile. "How could I forget? We looked like two drowned rats." Anamika laughed, her infectious mirth spreading to Karthik. "Or that time we accidentally swapped backpacks and ended up wearing each other's clothes?" The memory was a stark contrast to their current situation. Karthik couldn't help but laugh. As the stories unfolded, their shared laughter filled the park, a temporary reprieve from the weight of their decision.

In that moment, as they shared laughter and memories, a flicker of hope ignited. Perhaps, amidst the chaos of their lives, they could find a way to rebuild their friendship, to create a new chapter in their story.

Their laughter, like a gentle breeze, dispelled the heavy atmosphere that had enveloped them. The park, bathed in the warm glow of the setting sun, seemed to mirror the tentative warmth that was beginning to blossom between them.

As the laughter subsided, a comfortable silence settled between them. It was a shared silence, filled with unspoken understanding. Karthik reached out and took Anamika's hand, a silent acknowledgment of the fragile connection they were

rebuilding.

"I'm sorry for being so distant," he began, his voice barely audible. "I let my fear control me."

Anamika squeezed his hand. "We both made mistakes."

They sat in companionable silence, the gentle rustling of leaves providing a soothing backdrop to their conversation. In that moment, as they sat side by side, a sense of hope began to resurface. Perhaps, amidst the ruins of their shattered dreams, they could find the strength to rebuild.

A comfortable silence settled between them, the weight of their unspoken words hanging heavy in the air. The setting sun casts long, dancing shadows across the park, mirroring the complexity of their emotions.

Karthik reached out and took Anamika's hand, his touch gentle and reassuring. It was a silent promise, a vow to navigate the complexities of their relationship together.

"We can't let this define us," he began, his voice barely a whisper. "We're stronger than this."

Anamika squeezed his hand, her eyes filled with a newfound determination. "We are," she replied, her voice filled with a quiet strength.

As they sat in companionable silence, watching the sun disappear below the horizon, a sense of hope began to emerge. It was a fragile hope, a flicker of light in the darkness. But it was a start.

"I have to go to my hometown next week," Anamika said, her voice breaking the

comfortable silence. "My cousin's wedding."

A wave of disappointment washed over Karthik. The thought of spending a week without her was unbearable. But he nodded, understanding the inevitability of her absence.

"I'll miss you," he said, his voice filled with a quiet sadness.

Anamika squeezed his hand. "I'll miss you too," she replied, her eyes filled with a promise.

As they stood there, the setting sun casting a golden hue over the park, they made a silent vow. To cherish the moments they had, to build upon the fragile foundation they had laid. The future was uncertain, but for now, they were content with the promise of tomorrow.

CHAPTER - 7

KISS IN THE RAIN

The week without Anamika stretched like an endless desert. Each day was a barren expanse, devoid of her laughter, her touch, her presence. The once familiar campus seemed alien, a silent echo of their shared experiences.

Karthik found solace in their shared memories, replaying their conversations, their laughter, like a broken record. The love letter he had written, a physical manifestation of his feelings, lay untouched on his desk, a constant reminder of their shared journey.

The weight of her absence was a heavy burden, a constant ache in his heart. He spent countless hours alone, the quiet of his room a stark contrast to the vibrant chaos of the world outside. Yet, in the solitude, he found a strange clarity, a renewed determination to cherish the moments they had together.

Then came the day of her return. The campus seemed to come alive with anticipation. Karthik waited at the college gate, his heart pounding in his chest. When he saw her, a wave of relief washed over him. She looked tired, but her eyes held a familiar spark.

"I missed you," Karthik said, his voice filled with emotion.

Anamika smiled, her eyes sparkling. "I missed you too," she replied, her voice a soft melody.

As they walked towards the campus, the familiar surroundings seemed to come alive with renewed energy. The weight of their separation had cast a long shadow, but with her return, hope began to rekindle.

"I brought you something," Anamika said, pulling a small bag from her backpack. "Some sweets from the wedding."

Karthik's heart warmed at her gesture. It was a small thing, but it spoke volumes about their rekindled connection. "Let's go to my place," he suggested. "We can catch up properly."

Anamika nodded; her eyes filled with a quiet understanding. As they walked towards his apartment, a sense of anticipation filled the air. It was a new beginning.

A comfortable silence settled between them, the weight of their unspoken words hanging heavy in the air. The aroma of cardamom and saffron filled the room, a sweet counterpoint to the complexity of their emotions.

Karthik reached out and took Anamika's hand, his touch gentle and reassuring. It was a silent promise, a vow to navigate the complexities of their relationship together.

"I missed you," he began, his voice barely audible. "These past few days have been..." he trailed off, searching for the right words.

Anamika squeezed his hand, understanding the unspoken words. "I know," she replied, her voice filled with a quiet strength. "But we'll get through this."

A flicker of hope ignited within Karthik. It was a fragile flame, but it was there, a beacon in the darkness. He pulled her closer, their bodies a silent conversation. In that moment, as they sat in the quiet of his apartment, they found solace in each other's presence, a fragile foundation upon which they could rebuild their future. As the evening descended, casting long shadows through the apartment, a sense of peace settled between them. The initial tension had dissipated, replaced by a quiet companionship. They talked for hours, sharing stories, laughter, and dreams.

The soft glow of the table lamp created a warm ambiance, illuminating their faces. In the quiet intimacy of their shared moments, a connection began to rekindle, a fragile flame flickering to life.

As the night deepened, Anamika glanced at the clock. "It's getting late," she said, her voice filled with a hint of reluctance. "I should probably head back to the hostel."

Karthik felt a pang of disappointment. The evening had passed too quickly. He wanted to hold onto this moment, to prolong their shared silence. "Can't you stay?" he asked, his voice barely a whisper.

Anamika hesitated, her eyes filled with a mixture of desire and responsibility. "I wish I could," she replied, her voice soft. "But I have to be back."

As Anamika turned to leave, Karthik felt a pang of disappointment. The evening had been too short, their conversation leaving him wanting more. He wanted to spend every moment with her, to soak in her presence.

"Let me walk you back to your hostel," he offered, his voice filled with a quiet determination.

Anamika hesitated, a flicker of surprise crossing her face. "Are you sure?" she asked, her voice soft.

Karthik nodded, his heart pounding in his chest. "I want to spend more time with you," he replied, his voice barely a whisper.

As they walked through the campus, the night air was filled with the promise of a new beginning. The familiar surroundings seemed to come alive with a renewed energy, their shared presence casting a magical glow.

Suddenly, the sky opened up, and rain began to pour down. They sought shelter under the awning of a nearby tea shop, a familiar refuge from the elements. The warmth of the shop, coupled with the comforting aroma of tea, created a cozy atmosphere.

As they sat there, sipping their tea, the rain tapping against the windowpane, a sense of intimacy filled the air. The shared experience brought them closer, their bodies huddled together for warmth, their conversation a gentle murmur in the background.

The tea shop offered a respite from the relentless rain. As they sat closely on a bench, the warmth of their bodies seemed to defy the cold outside. The soft glow of the hanging lanterns cast an intimate ambiance, their reflections dancing in the pools of rainwater.

Anamika's laughter, a melody that had been missing from his world, filled the small space. As she spoke, her voice was a soothing balm to his soul. Karthik found himself drawn to her, the proximity a magnetic pull.

A subtle fragrance wafted towards him, a delicate blend of floral and musk. It was intoxicating, a sensory experience that awakened something deep within him. Curiosity piqued, he tilted his head slightly, bringing him closer to Anamika. His gaze fell upon her neck, the pulse point where the scent was most concentrated As Karthik leaned in, his breath mingling with the scent of her perfume, Anamika felt a surge of emotions. The proximity was intoxicating, a heady mix of desire and trepidation. Without conscious thought, she tilted her head towards him, her lips brushing against his in a fleeting touch.

Time seemed to stand still. Their hearts pounded in unison, a rhythm echoing the chaos within them. The world outside faded into insignificance, replaced by the intensity of their shared moment.

Their lips met again, this time with a deeper connection. It was a tentative exploration, a cautious dance of emotions. The rain outside seemed to mirror the storm within them, a tempest of passion and vulnerability.

The kiss, initiated with a tentative touch, quickly escalated into a passionate embrace. But just as quickly as it had begun, it ended. Anamika pulled away, her eyes wide with shock and anger.

Her hand, swift and sharp, connected with Karthik's cheek. The stinging sensation was a stark contrast to the warmth of their previous moment. "What do you think you're doing?" she demanded, her voice laced with fury.

Karthik was stunned. The euphoria of the moment had been shattered, replaced by a cold dread. "I'm sorry," he stammered, his voice barely a whisper. "I didn't mean to..."

Anamika's anger was palpable. "Didn't mean to? You kissed me without asking. That's not okay, Karthik." Her voice was rising, the words cutting through the silence like a knife.

The comfortable atmosphere of the tea shop had transformed into a battlefield, their shared intimacy replaced by a cold war. The rain outside seemed to mirror the storm raging within them.

CHAPTER - 8

KISSING AGAIN
WITH PERMISSION

Karthik felt a surge of regret. He had crossed a line, a boundary he should not have breached. But the desire to connect with her on a deeper level was overwhelming.

"I know," he began, his voice steady. "I crossed a line. I'm truly sorry. But I can't stop myself from wanting to kiss you." His voice was filled with a raw honesty. Anamika's anger began to subside, replaced by a flicker of understanding. She looked at him, her eyes filled with a mixture of confusion and desire. "I don't know," she whispered, her voice barely audible.

Without waiting for a response, Karthik reached out and gently cupped her face. His eyes met hers, a silent plea for forgiveness. "Can I kiss you? This time, I promise, I'll ask first."

Anamika hesitated, her heart pounding in her chest. The desire to resist was strong, but so was the pull towards him. With a deep breath, she nodded.

Karthik leaned in, his lips brushing against hers in a tender kiss. As the kiss deepened, a sense of intimacy filled the air, a connection that transcended words. The kiss deepened, a passionate exchange that seemed to consume them both. The world outside faded into insignificance, replaced by the intensity of their connection. But as the kiss deepened, Anamika pulled away, her breath coming in short gasps.

A look of fear crept into her eyes. "We have to stop," she said, her voice trembling. "I need to go."

Karthik was caught off guard by her sudden change of heart. The euphoria of the moment was replaced by a sense of confusion. "But it's raining," he protested, his voice filled with disappointment.

Anamika shook her head, her determination unwavering. "I know, but I have to go," she repeated, her voice firm.

As she stood up, she reached out and touched his face, her fingers lingering on his skin. "Don't worry," she said, her voice soft. "This isn't goodbye."

With that, she turned and walked out into the rain, disappearing into the night. Karthik was left alone, the warmth of their shared moment replaced by a cold emptiness. The rain outside seemed to mirror the storm raging within him.

The rain continued to pour, creating a soothing rhythm against the windowpane. Karthik watched as Anamika walked away, her figure disappearing into the night. The warmth of their shared moment was replaced by a cold emptiness.

He returned to his apartment, the familiar surroundings offering little solace. The rain outside mirrored the storm raging within him. The kiss, a fleeting moment of intimacy, had left him with a longing that was both exhilarating and painful.

He replayed the events of the evening in his mind, the touch of her lips, the warmth of her body. It was a bittersweet memory, a reminder of the complexities of their relationship. The uncertainty of their future was a heavy burden, but the hope that flickered between them was a beacon in the darkness.

The morning sun filtered through the classroom windows, casting long shadows on the desks. Students trickled in, their voices a low hum in the otherwise quiet room. Karthik took his usual seat, his gaze scanning the room. His heart pounded in his chest as he waited for Anamika to arrive.

When she finally entered the classroom, their eyes met. Anamika's face flushed, and she quickly lowered her head, avoiding his gaze. The memory of the previous night's events was a fresh wound, a reminder of the complexities of their relationship.

Karthik felt a pang of disappointment. He wanted to reach out, to offer comfort, but the fear of rejection held him back. Instead, he focused on the lecture, his mind wandering to the previous night's events. The echo of their shared laughter and the intensity of their kiss were a stark contrast to the sterile environment of the classroom.

Anamika's eyes met his, a silent acknowledgment of the tension between them. The classroom, once a neutral space, had transformed into a battlefield of unspoken emotions. The soft murmur of her classmates seemed to amplify the silence between them.

Karthik felt a surge of frustration. He wanted to reach out, to bridge the gap between them, but the fear of rejection held him back. Instead, he focused on the lecture, his mind wandering to the previous night's events.

The memory of their shared intimacy was a bittersweet reminder of the complexities of their relationship. He longed for a resolution, a way to move forward. But as he looked at Anamika, he realized that the path ahead was uncertain.

The classroom was a blur of textbooks and lecture notes. Karthik's mind, however, was far from the subject matter. The memory of the previous night's encounter with Anamika was a constant undercurrent, a bittersweet reminder of their complex relationship.

He was jolted back to reality by a familiar voice. "Karthik, any advice for a hopeless romantic?" Anvesh, his ever-cheerful friend, was standing beside his desk, a mischievous glint in his eye.

Karthik managed a weak smile. "What's up, Anvesh?"

"It's Ria," Anvesh explained, his voice filled with a mix of excitement and nervousness. "I'm planning a surprise date for her. Need your expert opinion."

Karthik chuckled, trying to shake off the lingering melancholy. "Expert opinion, huh? Alright, let's hear your plan."

As Anvesh outlined his ideas, Karthik found himself lost in thought. Watching his friend navigate the complexities of love brought a strange sense of peace. Perhaps, in helping

Anvesh, he could find a temporary escape from his own emotional turmoil.

"So, I was thinking of a picnic in the park," Anvesh continued, his eyes sparkling with anticipation. "We could lay out a blanket, some snacks, maybe even a bottle of wine."

Karthik nodded, a smile playing on his lips. It was a classic, romantic idea. "That's a great start," he said. "But don't forget the little details."

"Like what?" Anvesh asked, eager for more input.

"Create an ambiance," Karthik suggested. "Soft music, maybe a few candles if it's not too windy. And personalize it. Think about things Ria loves. Maybe a book she's reading, a movie you both enjoyed. Little touches like that can make a big difference."

Anvesh's eyes lit up. "That's a great idea," he said, jotting down notes on his phone. "And maybe, just maybe, a surprise at the end."

"A surprise?" Karthik mused, leaning back in his chair. "Now, that's where the magic happens. Make it unexpected, something she wouldn't see coming."

Anvesh nodded enthusiastically. "I was thinking maybe a personalized message, like a video or something. Or maybe a small gift, something she really wants."

Karthik smiled. "That's a good start. But remember, it's not just about the gift. It's about the emotion behind it. Make it personal, make it meaningful."

Anvesh's eyes lit up with excitement. "I've got it," he declared. "I'll combine both. A personalized video with a small, but meaningful gift. It'll be perfect."

Karthik gave him an encouraging pat on the back. "I have no doubt about that. You're going to blow her away."

As the lecture drew to a close, Anvesh's excitement was palpable. He had spent the entire class refining his plan, and now, it was time to put it into action. Turning to Ria, he flashed her a charming smile. "So, I was thinking," he began, his voice laced with anticipation, "maybe we could go to the park later tonight? Just the two of us."

Ria's face lit up with surprise. "A date?" she teased, a playful glint in her eye. Anvesh nodded, his heart pounding in his chest. "A proper date," he confirmed, his voice filled with determination. "I've got something special planned."

Ria's curiosity was piqued. She hesitated for a moment, her mind racing with possibilities. Finally, a mischievous grin spread across her face. "Alright, let's do it," she agreed.

As the final bell rang, signaling the end of the class, Anvesh felt a surge of excitement. The stage was set, and he was ready to make it a night to remember. As the sun began its descent, casting long shadows across the park, Anvesh arrived, his heart pounding with anticipation. Ria, dressed in a flowy summer

dress, was waiting for him, a smile playing on her lips.

They spread out a checkered blanket on the soft grass, the city lights twinkling in the distance. Anvesh had brought along a picnic basket filled with their favorite snacks and a bottle of wine. As they shared laughter and stories, the atmosphere was filled with a sense of intimacy.

After a while, Anvesh pulled out his phone. "I have something to show you," he said, his voice filled with excitement. He played a video he had created, a montage of their shared memories, set to a soft, romantic soundtrack. Ria's eyes welled up with tears as she watched the video, a testament to their growing bond. At the end of the video, a message appeared on the screen: "Will you be my partner in this crazy adventure called life?"

Anvesh took a deep breath. "Ria, I know this isn't the most romantic proposal, but I mean every word. Will you be my girlfriend?"

Ria's heart was pounding in her chest. She looked at Anvesh, her eyes filled with love and admiration. "Yes," she whispered, her voice barely audible.

As they shared their first kiss, the world around them seemed to fade away. The park, once a familiar space, had transformed into a magical realm, filled with the promise of a future together.

As the first stars began to twinkle in the night sky, a comfortable silence settled between Anvesh and Ria. The intensity of the moment had subsided, replaced by a gentle warmth.

Anvesh, breaking the silence, spoke softly. "You know, I've had my heart broken a few times before." His voice was laced with a hint of melancholy. "I used to think love was just a temporary high, something that faded with time."

Ria's hand found his, offering silent comfort. "But you found me," she said, her voice filled with hope.

Anvesh squeezed her hand. "And I'm so glad I did. You've shown me that love can be something more than just a fleeting emotion. It's a commitment, a partnership."

The night air was filled with the promise of something new, a future painted with hues of hope and uncertainty. Anvesh and Ria sat on the park bench, their bodies close, their hearts even closer. The soft glow of the city lights cast an ethereal glow on their faces, illuminating their shared dreams.

Anvesh continued, his voice low, "I used to think love was a distraction, something that hindered my ambitions. But you've shown me that love can be a source of strength, a catalyst for growth."

Ria squeezed his hand, her heart filled with a warmth she hadn't felt in a long time. "We're still at the beginning of our journey," she said softly. "But I know we can face anything together."

A comfortable silence settled between them, the only sound the gentle rustling of leaves. The park, once a mere backdrop to their lives, had transformed into a sacred space, a witness to their growing love.

As the night deepened, they shared stories, laughter, and dreams. Anvesh talked about his aspirations, his hopes for the future. Ria listened intently, her eyes filled with admiration. She shared her fears, her insecurities, her hopes for a career in medicine.

In the quiet intimacy of their shared moments, they found solace and strength.

The weight of the world seemed to disappear, replaced by the simple joy of being together. They talked about everything and nothing, their conversation flowing effortlessly.

As the clock struck midnight, a sense of reluctance filled the air. They had lost track of time, immersed in each other's company. The world outside seemed to fade into insignificance.

"I don't want this night to end," Anvesh said, his voice filled with regret. Ria smiled, her eyes sparkling. "Me neither," she replied.

They stood up, their bodies reluctant to separate. As they walked towards the exit, the night air felt crisp and refreshing. The city lights, once a distant blur, now seemed to hold a promise of endless possibilities.

"I'll walk you home," Karthik offered, his voice filled with gentle determination. Anamika nodded, a silent agreement. As they walked through the quiet streets, their hands brushed against each other, a silent conversation filled with unspoken promises.

When they reached Anamika's hostel, they stood at the gate, the night air filled with a bittersweet silence. "I'll see you tomorrow," Karthik said, his voice filled with hope.

Anamika smiled. "I can't wait," she replied.

As she turned to leave, Karthik reached out and held her hand. Their eyes met, a silent promise passing between them. With a final squeeze, he let go, watching as she disappeared into the night.

The walk back to his apartment was filled with a sense of peace and contentment. The night had been magical, a turning point in their relationship. As he slipped into bed, a smile crept across his face.

CHAPTER - 9

DOUBLE DATE

The evening arrived, and with it, a nervous anticipation. Karthik had booked a table at his family's five-star restaurant, a place he rarely visited. The grandeur of the place was a stark contrast to the casual atmosphere they were used to. But he wanted to make this night special.

Anamika arrived, looking stunning in a simple yet elegant dress. Her presence lit up the room, her laughter mingling with the soft clinking of silverware. Anvesh and Ria joined them, their excitement palpable.

The dinner was a blend of delicious food, witty conversations, and shared laughter. As the night progressed, the initial awkwardness faded, replaced by a comfortable camaraderie. Karthik found himself drawn to Anamika, their eyes meeting across the table, a silent conversation filled with unspoken promises.

Anvesh and Ria, oblivious to the undercurrents between Karthik and Anamika, were lost in their own world. Their laughter filled the room, a contagious melody that added to the warmth of the evening.

As the night drew to a close, they stepped out into the cool night air. The city lights twinkled like distant stars, casting a magical glow over the bustling metropolis.

"This was amazing," Ria said, her voice filled with gratitude. "Thank you for inviting us."

Karthik smiled. "It was my pleasure," he replied.

Anvesh turned to Anamika, his eyes filled with admiration. "You look stunning tonight," he said, his voice laced with sincerity.

Anamika blushed, her eyes sparkling with happiness. "Thank you," she replied, her voice soft.

As they stood there, the four of them, a silent understanding passed between Karthik and Anamika. It was a moment of connection, a promise of something more.

As the night drew to a close, it was time to part ways. Anvesh and Ria hailed a cab, their laughter echoing in the night air. Karthik and Anamika stood on the sidewalk, the city lights casting long shadows over them.

"I had a great time," Anamika said, her voice filled with a hint of sadness. Karthik nodded, his heart heavy. "Me too," he replied, his voice barely a whisper. As she turned to leave, he reached out and took her hand. "Can I see you tomorrow?" he asked, his voice filled with hope.

Anamika hesitated, her eyes filled with a mixture of desire and fear.

Finally, she nodded. "I'd like that," she replied, her voice barely audible.

As she walked away, Karthik watched her until she disappeared from sight. The night air was filled with a sense of anticipation, a promise of what was to come. He returned to his apartment, his mind racing with thoughts of Anamika. The evening had been a turning point, a step forward in their complex relationship.

Karthik returned to the city, his mind a whirlwind of emotions. The revelation about his past had shaken him to the core, but it had also given him a newfound strength. He knew he had to focus on the present, on Anamika, and on their shared future.

Anamika was waiting for him, her face etched with concern. "Where were you?" she asked, her voice filled with worry.

Karthik hesitated, the lie forming on his lips. "I had to take care of something personal," he replied, his voice steady. The guilt gnawed at him, but he couldn't risk revealing the truth just yet.

Anamika nodded, her eyes filled with understanding. "I hope everything is okay," she said softly.

Karthik forced a smile. "It is," he assured her. "Don't worry about it."

The lie hung heavy in the air, a silent barrier between them. But they both understood the unspoken agreement. Some things were better left unsaid.

The days that followed were a blur of study and stolen moments. The impending exams cast a long shadow over their lives, but their love for each other was a beacon of hope in the darkness. They studied together, their shared goals bringing them closer.

One evening, as they sat in the library, surrounded by stacks of textbooks, Anamika broke the silence. "I've been thinking," she began, her voice filled with a mixture of excitement and trepidation. "What if we take a break after exams? A small vacation, maybe? Just the two of us."

Karthik's heart skipped a beat. The idea of a vacation with Anamika was intoxicating. It was a chance to escape the pressures of their lives, to focus solely on each other.

"I'd love that," he replied, his voice filled with enthusiasm. "We can go somewhere quiet, where we can just relax and enjoy each other's company."

Anamika smiled, her eyes sparkling with excitement. "I know just the place," she said, her voice filled with a sense of adventure.

As they discussed potential destinations, their laughter filled the library, a stark contrast to the quiet intensity of their studies. In that moment, they forgot about the looming exams, lost in the dream of a future together.

The countdown to exams is a constant reminder of the challenges ahead. But their love for each other was a source of strength, a beacon of hope during the storm. They supported each other, studied together, and created memories that would last a lifetime.

The exam hall was a silent battleground, each student a solitary warrior fighting for academic supremacy. Karthik, armed with knowledge and a quiet determination, tackled the questions with focused intensity. The memory of Anamika's support, her belief in his abilities, fueled his determination.

When the final exam ended, a sense of liberation washed over him. The weeks of intense study had paid off. As he stepped out of the examination hall, he felt a surge of accomplishment. He had done it. The grueling journey of medical school

was nearing its end.

With the exams over, a sense of freedom washed over him. He decided to visit his uncle, a gesture of gratitude and a way to connect with a part of his past he had long neglected. The journey was a time for reflection, a chance to process the whirlwind of emotions he had experienced in recent weeks.

Upon reaching his uncle's house, he was greeted with a warm embrace. His uncle looked visibly relieved, his eyes filled with a mixture of concern and pride. They spent the evening catching up, the conversation flowing effortlessly. Karthik learned more about his uncle's life, his struggles, and his unwavering dedication to protecting his family.

The following days were a blur of activity. Karthik helped his uncle with the business, gaining a deeper understanding of the world his parents had once inhabited. It was a challenging experience, but it was also a rewarding one. He felt a sense of purpose, a connection to his roots that he had never experienced before.

Anamika called almost every day, her voice a constant source of comfort. They talked about their plans for the future, about their dreams, and about their love for each other. The distance between them seemed to shrink with each conversation, their bond deepening with every passing day.

The day of the results arrived, a mix of anticipation and fear. Karthik and his friends gathered together, their hearts pounding in their chests. When the results were finally announced, they had all passed with flying colors. The collective

sigh of relief was followed by an eruption of joy.

The celebration that night was a blur of laughter, music, and shared dreams. Karthik and Anamika danced the night away, their bodies moving in perfect synchrony. The world seemed to disappear, replaced by the magic of their shared moment.

As the night ended, Karthik walked Anamika home. The city lights cast a romantic glow over the quiet streets. They stood at her doorstep, the moment stretched between them.

"Thank you," Anamika said, her voice filled with gratitude. "For everything." Karthik smiled. "Thank you for being you," he replied, his heart full.

They shared a long, lingering kiss, a promise of a future filled with love and happiness. As Anamika turned to leave, Karthik felt a sense of peace he hadn't experienced in a long time. The journey had been challenging, but the destination was worth it.

CHAPTER - 10

THIRD YEAR

The third year of medical school was a whirlwind of clinical rotations and increasing responsibilities. Yet, amidst the demanding schedule, Karthik found solace in Anamika's unwavering support. Their relationship had deepened, their love a steady beacon in the stormy seas of medical life.

As the batch seniors, they were tasked with organizing the welcome party for the freshers. It was a daunting responsibility, but also an exciting challenge. Karthik and Anamika worked tirelessly, their shared passion for the event bringing them closer together.

The party night arrived, a kaleidoscope of colors, music, and youthful energy. As they welcomed the freshers, Karthik caught a glimpse of a girl standing by the refreshment table. She was strikingly beautiful, with a confidence that belied her young age. Her name was Hasmitha, a first-year medical student.

Hasmitha was drawn to Karthik's quiet charm and enigmatic aura. There was something about him that set him apart from the crowd. As the night progressed, they found themselves engaged in a conversation, their connection growing with each passing moment.

Days turned into weeks, and their friendship deepened. Hasmitha, with her infectious laughter and vibrant personality, brought a fresh energy to Karthik's life. He found himself looking forward to their interactions, their conversations a welcome respite from the rigors of medical school.

One evening, as they sat together in the library, studying for an upcoming exam, Hasmitha confessed her feelings for him. "I know this is sudden, and I understand if you don't feel the same way," she began, her voice filled with a mix of hope and trepidation. "But I can't deny how I feel about you."

Karthik was taken aback. He had developed a deep affection for Hasmitha, but his heart belonged to Anamika. He had to be honest with her, even if it meant breaking her heart.

"Hasmitha, I appreciate your feelings," he began, his voice filled with sincerity. "You're an amazing person, and I value our friendship immensely. But my heart belongs to someone else."

Hasmitha's face fell, but she nodded, understanding the finality of his words. "I understand," she said, her voice barely a whisper.

The following days were awkward, the tension between them palpable. Karthik felt guilty for hurting her feelings, but he knew he had made the right decision. His loyalty to Anamika was unwavering.

As the final exams approached, the pressure mounted. Karthik and Anamika spent countless hours together, studying and supporting each other. Their love for each other was a source of strength, a beacon of hope in the midst of the academic storm.

The day of the final exam arrived, a mix of anticipation and fear. As they entered the examination hall, they held hands, a silent pact of support. The exam was grueling, but they faced it together, their love for each other a shield against the pressure.

When the final exam ended, a sense of liberation washed over them. They had done it. The grueling journey of medical school was nearing its end. As they stepped out of the examination hall, they shared a long, passionate kiss, a celebration of their shared victory.

The future was uncertain, filled with both hopes and fears. But as they stood there, hand in hand, they knew that they would face whatever challenges came their way together. Their love was a foundation, a solid ground upon which they could build their future.

The final exam was a blur of questions and answers. As Karthik stepped out of the examination hall, a sense of liberation washed over him. The grueling journey of medical school was nearing its end. Anamika was waiting for him, her eyes filled with a mixture of relief and anticipation.

"We did it," she said, her voice filled with a sense of accomplishment.

Karthik nodded, his heart filled with a quiet pride. They had faced the challenges together, their love a constant source of strength.

As they walked through the campus, the setting sun cast long shadows, creating an ethereal atmosphere. The weight of the exams, a burden they had carried for weeks, seemed to lift, replaced by a sense of freedom.

"To celebrate," Karthik began, his voice filled with a hint of excitement, "how about dinner at that new Italian place downtown?"

Anamika's eyes lit up. "I'd love to," she replied, her voice filled with anticipation. The restaurant was a blend of modern elegance and old-world charm. As they were seated, Karthik couldn't help but feel a sense of gratitude. Anamika had been his constant support, his rock through the storms of medical school.

The conversation flowed effortlessly, a mix of laughter and shared dreams. They talked about their plans for the future, about the challenges they had overcome, and about the love that had sustained them. As the night deepened, the restaurant filled with the soft glow of candlelight, creating an intimate atmosphere.

After dinner, they walked along the riverfront, the cool night air refreshing their senses. The city lights reflected on the water, creating a magical ambiance. They shared stories, laughter, and secrets, their connection deepening with each passing moment.

As they reached Anamika's hostel, the reluctance to part ways was palpable. Karthik wanted to spend more time with her, to lose himself in the warmth of her presence.

"Can I see you tomorrow?" he asked, his voice filled with hope.

Anamika nodded, her eyes filled with a silent promise. "I'd like that," she replied. As they stood there, the night air filled with a sense of anticipation, Karthik reached out and took her hand. Their fingers intertwined, a silent connection between their hearts. With a final, lingering look, Anamika turned and walked away, disappearing into the night.

Karthik stood there for a long time, watching her retreating figure. The night was filled with a sense of peace and contentment. He had found love, a love that had weathered the storms of their lives. As he walked back to his apartment, he couldn't shake the feeling that something special was about to happen.

The following day, as the city woke up to a new day, Karthik felt a sense of anticipation. The thought of seeing Anamika filled him with a warmth that was unfamiliar yet comforting. He spent the morning preparing breakfast, setting the stage for a perfect day.

When Anamika arrived, she was greeted by the aroma of freshly brewed coffee and the sight of a beautifully set table. Her eyes lit up with surprise and delight. They spent the morning talking, laughing, and simply enjoying each other's company. As the day wore on, the atmosphere in the apartment shifted, the air filled with a charged tension.

Karthik moved closer to Anamika, his heart pounding in his chest. Their eyes met, a silent conversation filled with unspoken desires. Slowly, he reached out and took her hand, his touch gentle and reassuring.

Anamika's breath quickened, her eyes filled with a mix of fear and anticipation. She wanted to resist, but the pull towards him was undeniable. As their lips met, the world around them faded away, replaced by the intensity of their connection. The kiss deepened, a passionate exploration of their desires. Their bodies moved in synchrony, their hearts beating as one. The world outside seemed to disappear, replaced by the intimate universe they had created.

As the afternoon wore on, their passion cooled into a tender affection. They lay in each other's arms, the gentle rhythm of their breathing filling the room. The outside world seemed irrelevant, their focus solely on the moment, on the connection they shared.

In that moment, as they lay together, surrounded by the warmth of their love, Karthik felt a sense of completeness he had never experienced before. He had found his home, his safe harbor, in the arms of the woman he loved.

The morning sun filtered through the curtains, casting a warm glow on their faces. Anamika stirred, her eyes slowly opening to reveal a world bathed in soft light. Karthik was still asleep, his face relaxed in slumber, a picture of contentment.

A wave of contentment washed over her. She had spent the night in his arms, a night filled with intimacy and a sense of belonging. It was a night she would cherish forever.

As she got out of bed, she moved quietly, not wanting to disturb his peaceful sleep. She prepared breakfast, the aroma of coffee filling the apartment. When she returned to the bedroom, Karthik was awake, his eyes still heavy with sleep. "Good morning," she said, her voice soft.

He smiled, pulling her into a gentle hug. "Morning," he replied, his voice filled with sleepiness.

They spent the morning in each other's company, the world outside a distant blur. As the day wore on, the realization of the impending separation began to cast a

shadow over their happiness.

"I have to go back to my hometown tomorrow," Anamika said, her voice filled with a hint of sadness.

Karthik's heart sank. The thought of spending another day apart was unbearable. "Can't you stay a little longer?" he asked, his voice filled with hope.

Anamika shook her head, her eyes filled with a mixture of sadness and determination. "I have to be there for my family," she explained.

Karthik nodded, understanding the weight of her responsibilities. "I'll miss you," he said, his voice filled with a quiet sadness.

Anamika reached out and took his hand. "I'll miss you too," she replied, her voice barely a whisper.

As the day drew to a close, they stood at the door, the weight of their impending separation heavy in the air. Karthik pulled Anamika into a long, lingering hug, the warmth of her body a comforting presence.

"I'll call you," he promised, his voice filled with a sense of hope.

Anamika nodded, her eyes filled with tears. "I can't wait," she replied, her voice barely audible.

With a final, lingering look, she turned and left, disappearing into the night. Karthik stood there for a long time, watching as her figure disappeared from sight. The apartment, once filled with the warmth of their shared presence, now felt cold and empty.

The days following Anamika's departure were a blur of loneliness and routine.

Karthik found himself reaching for his phone incessantly, his thumb hovering over her contact, only to hesitate at the last moment. The silence that greeted him was deafening, a stark contrast to the symphony of their conversations.

Work became a distraction, a way to escape the gnawing emptiness within. He immersed himself in his uncle's business, finding solace in the structured routine. The familiar surroundings of the office provided a temporary respite from the storm raging within him.

Nights were the worst. The quiet of his apartment amplified the absence of Anamika. Every sound, every shadow, was a reminder of her absence. He would lie awake for hours, replaying their shared moments, their laughter, their dreams. The hope that had once fueled him was now replaced by a creeping despair.

Days turned into weeks, and still, there was no word from Anamika. The silence between them was a tangible presence, a constant reminder of the distance between them. Karthik began to doubt if he would ever hear from her again.

The fear of losing her was a constant companion. He found himself replaying their conversations, searching for clues, for any hint of what might have caused her silence. But there were no answers, only questions.

To distract himself, Karthik threw himself into his work. He spent long hours at the office, immersing himself in the complexities of the business. The challenge of it all provided a temporary escape from the pain of his loneliness.

Yet, as the days turned into weeks, the weight of his longing for Anamika began to wear him down. He missed her laughter, her support, her presence. The world seemed to have lost its color, replaced by a monochromatic palette of loneliness and despair.

CHAPTER - 11

FINAL YEAR

The final year of medical school loomed large, a daunting horizon filled with the promise of both challenges and triumphs. For Karthik and Anamika, it was a time of both anticipation and apprehension. They were on the cusp of their professional lives, yet their personal relationship was still evolving.

Anamika, with her characteristic directness, broached the subject one evening as they sat in the familiar comfort of Karthik's apartment. "I've been thinking," she began, her voice filled with a mixture of nervousness and excitement, "about moving in."

Karthik's heart skipped a beat. The thought of living with Anamika had crossed his mind countless times, but he hadn't dared to voice it. "Really?" he managed to say, his voice barely a whisper.

Anamika nodded, her eyes filled with a determination that surprised him. "I know it's sudden, but I think it would make things easier. We could study together, support each other, and, well, just be together."

Karthik felt a surge of happiness. Living with Anamika was something he had secretly longed for. It was a step towards a future they had both imagined. "I'd like that," he said, his voice filled with a sense of anticipation.

The decision to move in together was a turning point in their relationship. It was a leap of faith, a testament to the trust and love they shared. As Anamika started packing her belongings, a wave of excitement and nervousness washed over Karthik. Their shared space was about to become a canvas for their shared future.

The apartment, once a solitary space, began to transform. Anamika brought a touch of her personality to the decor, infusing the room with warmth and life. Their personal belongings intertwined, creating a space that was uniquely theirs. Living together was a beautiful chaos. They studied together, cooked together, and laughed together. The mundane tasks of everyday life became a shared adventure, their love a constant source of strength. They supported each other through the challenges of medical school, their bond deepening with each

passing day.

Yet, amidst the joy and companionship, there were moments of vulnerability. The intensity of their relationship, the constant proximity, brought to the surface unspoken fears and insecurities. There were disagreements, moments of frustration, but they navigated these challenges with a newfound maturity.

Their love story was an evolving tapestry, woven with threads of joy, challenges, and unwavering support. As they stood on the precipice of their medical careers, their relationship was a solid foundation, a promise of a future filled with love, laughter, and endless possibilities.

As the weeks turned into months, the lines between friendship and love blurred. Living together brought an intimacy that went beyond physical proximity. They shared laughter, tears, dreams, and fears, their bond deepening with each passing day.

Karthik found himself falling deeper in love with Anamika. Her strength, her resilience, and her unwavering support were a constant source of inspiration. He had forgotten the initial terms of their relationship, the carefully constructed boundaries that were meant to protect their hearts.

One evening, as they were cooking dinner together, the conversation drifted to their future. "I can't imagine my life without you," Karthik said, his voice filled with a sense of certainty.

Anamika smiled, her eyes filled with a warmth that melted away the last vestiges of their carefully constructed walls. "Neither can I," she replied, her voice soft.

In that moment, the future seemed filled with endless possibilities. They talked about buying a house, about having children, about growing old together. It was a conversation born out of love, a testament to the depth of their connection.

However, amidst the euphoria of their shared dreams, a nagging doubt crept into Karthik's mind. He remembered the conditions Anamika had imposed, the rules they had agreed upon. He had broken those rules, and he was afraid of the consequences.

He hesitated, his mind racing. Should he tell her about his feelings, or should he continue to live in this blissful ignorance? The fear of rejection was a constant companion, but so was the desire for honesty.

The decision was not easy. But as he looked at Anamika, her laughter filling the room, he knew that he couldn't live with the lie. He had to be honest, no matter the consequences.

"There's something I need to tell you," he began, his voice filled with a mixture of hope and fear.

Karthik's voice trembled slightly as he continued, "Remember when you said we should keep our relationship within the confines of medical school?" A wave of silence washed over the room, the weight of his words hanging heavy in the air.

Anamika's face paled, her eyes wide with shock. She had tried to forget those conditions, to focus on the love they shared. But now, they were a stark reminder of the fragile foundation upon which their relationship was built.

"I know I broke that promise," Karthik confessed, his voice filled with regret. "I fell in love with you, and I couldn't let go."

Anamika's heart pounded in her chest. She had hoped to ignore the rules they had set, to believe that their love could conquer all. But now, faced with the reality of their situation, she felt a pang of despair.

"I know," she replied, her voice barely a whisper. "I did too."

A heavy silence settled between them, the weight of their unspoken words hanging heavy in the air. The room, once filled with warmth and intimacy, now felt cold and empty.

Karthik reached out and took her hand, his touch a silent plea for understanding. "I don't want to lose you," he said, his voice filled with desperation. "I love you, more than words can say."

Anamika pulled her hand away, her eyes filled with a mixture of sadness and anger. "We can't ignore the rules, Karthik," she said, her voice firm. "We made a promise." And the promises are made to be kept.

The words were like a cold shower, dousing the flames of their hope.

Karthik's composure shattered. The carefully constructed facade of resilience crumbled, revealing the raw pain beneath. Tears streamed down his face, a silent testament to the depth of his despair. "Why is this happening to us?" he cried out, his voice filled with anguish.

Anamika was taken aback by the intensity of his emotion. She reached out to him, her hand trembling. "I know," she whispered, her voice filled with sorrow. "I wish things were different."

Karthik pulled her into a tight embrace, his body shaking with sobs. The weight of their situation was overwhelming, a crushing burden that seemed to consume them both. Anamika held him tightly, her arms offering a sense of comfort and security. She stroked his hair, whispering words of encouragement. Slowly, the intensity of his emotions began to subside, replaced by a weary resignation.

"We'll get through this," she said, her voice filled with a quiet determination. "Together."

Karthik nodded, his voice barely a whisper. "I hope so," he replied.

Anamika knew that words were not enough. She needed to distract him, to take his mind off the pain. With a mischievous glint in her eye, she leaned in and kissed him softly.

The kiss was a gentle balm to his wounded heart. It was a reminder of the love they shared, a beacon of hope in the darkness. As the kiss deepened, their bodies moved in synchrony, their passion a temporary escape from the harsh realities of life.

In that moment, as they held each other tight, they found solace in each other's arms. The world outside seemed to fade away, replaced by the intimacy of their shared moment. It was a fragile hope, a flicker of light in the darkness, but it was enough to keep them going.

The kiss deepened, a passionate exploration of their desires. The world outside seemed to fade away, replaced by the intensity of their connection. As their bodies moved in synchrony, a sense of peace washed over them. It was in these moments of intimacy that they found solace, a refuge from the storms of life.

But as the initial passion subsided, a pang of reality struck Karthik. Anamika's words about her impending marriage echoed in his mind. The happiness they had shared was a fleeting moment, a beautiful illusion in the face of their harsh reality.

Anamika, sensing his shift in mood, pulled away slightly. Her eyes held a mixture of concern and understanding. "I'm sorry," she whispered, her voice filled with regret. "I didn't mean to upset you."

Karthik forced a smile. "It's okay," he replied, his voice steady. "I just... I wasn't expecting it to hit me so hard."

They sat in silence for a moment, the weight of their situation hanging heavy in the air. Anamika reached out and took his hand, her touch a silent promise of support.

"We'll get through this," she said, her voice filled with a quiet determination. "Together."

Karthik nodded, his heart heavy. He knew she was right. They had to face the future, no matter how painful it might be.

Days turned into weeks, the countdown to Anamika's wedding drawing closer. Karthik tried to put on a brave face, but the pain of losing her was a constant companion. He threw himself into his studies, hoping to find solace in the familiar routine.

The wedding day arrived, a stark reminder of the end of their chapter.

Karthik attended the ceremony, a ghost in the crowd. As he watched Anamika exchange vows with her fiancé, a wave of grief washed over him. He had loved her with a passion that consumed him, and now, she was beginning a new life without him.

The reception was a blur of faces and forced smiles. Karthik managed to maintain a semblance of normalcy, but his heart was breaking. As the night drew to a close, he found himself alone, the weight of his loss a heavy burden.

He walked through the deserted streets, the city lights a stark contrast to the darkness within him. The rain began to fall, a cold and unforgiving companion. He let it wash over him, cleansing his soul of the pain and sorrow.

As he reached his apartment, he collapsed on the bed, the weight of his loss finally overwhelming him. The future, once filled with hope and promise, now seemed bleak and uncertain. But in the depths of his despair, he found a flicker of resilience. He would survive this, he told himself. He would find a way to move on.

CHAPTER - 12

WITHOUT HER

The days turned into weeks, each one a painful reminder of Anamika's absence. Karthik found it increasingly difficult to cope with the void she had left. The once vibrant world had turned into a monochromatic canvas, devoid of color and joy.

Desperation crept into his life. The weight of his loneliness became unbearable. In the darkest hours of the night, when the world was silent, he was consumed by thoughts of ending the pain.

One evening, as darkness enveloped the city, Karthik stood on the edge of despair. The world seemed to have lost its meaning, replaced by a profound emptiness. In a moment of weakness, he made a decision that would change everything.

Anamika, meanwhile, was basking in the newlywed bliss. The world was a kaleidoscope of colors, filled with laughter and love. Her honeymoon was a dream come true, a perfect escape from the complexities of life. Little did she know, the man she had left behind was on the brink of despair.

Back in the city, the ambulance sirens wailed through the night, breaking the silence. Karthik lay on the cold, hard floor, the world fading to black. As consciousness slipped away, he thought of Anamika, a final flicker of hope in the darkness.

The hospital room was filled with the low hum of machines and the soft chatter of nurses. Karthik lay in bed, his mind a fog of confusion and despair. The events of the past few days had taken a toll on him, leaving him physically and emotionally drained.

The door opened, and Karthik's uncle entered the room. His face was etched with concern. "How are you feeling, son?" he asked, his voice filled with genuine care.

Karthik managed a weak smile. "I'm okay," he replied, his voice barely a whisper.

His uncle sat down beside the bed, his hand resting gently on Karthik's arm. "I've spoken to your friends," he said. "They told me everything."

Karthik closed his eyes, the pain of the past few days resurfacing. He had tried to protect Anamika from the turmoil of his life, but in the end, it had affected them both.

"I'm so sorry," his uncle said, his voice filled with empathy. "I should have been there for you."

Karthik shook his head. "It's not your fault," he replied, his voice filled with a sense of resignation.

His uncle reached out and squeezed his hand. "I want to help you, Karthik.

I know this is a difficult time, but you need to focus on healing."

Karthik nodded, his heart heavy. He knew his uncle was right. He needed to move on, to find a way to rebuild his life.

A few days later, Karthik was discharged from the hospital. The physical wounds were healing, but the emotional scars ran deep. He returned to his apartment, a place filled with memories of Anamika. Every corner of the room seemed to echo with her absence.

To escape the haunting memories, he decided to take a break. He asked his uncle for a transfer to a different hospital, hoping that a change of environment would help him heal. His uncle, understanding his need for a fresh start, agreed to the transfer.

The new hospital was a world away from his familiar surroundings. The unfamiliar faces, the different routines, provided a much-needed distraction. He immersed himself in his work, hoping to find solace in the routine of his profession.

The decision to pursue a PG in cardiology was a desperate attempt to escape the haunting memories. It was a way to immerse himself in something demanding, to numb the pain with the rigors of academic pursuit.

As he boarded the plane, a wave of loneliness washed over him. He was leaving behind everything familiar, everything that connected him to Anamika. The city, once filled with the echoes of their shared laughter, now seemed like a distant memory.

The new country was a stark contrast to the life he had left behind. The language barrier, the unfamiliar culture, and the demanding course work created a protective shield around him. He immersed himself in studies, hoping to find solace in the pursuit of knowledge.

Months turned into years. Karthik transformed into a dedicated doctor, his work becoming an escape from the pain of the past. Yet, the void in his heart remained. Nights were the hardest, the silence of his apartment a stark reminder of the loneliness he had carried with him.

He lost contact with most of his friends, including Anvesh and Hasmitha. The distance, coupled with the demands of his new life, had created an insurmountable barrier. It was as if he had erased a significant part of his past, leaving behind only fragments of memories.

One evening, while on duty, he received a call from an unknown number. It was a hospital in India. The news was devastating. Anvesh had met with an accident. Karthik felt a surge of panic, a familiar dread creeping into his heart. He booked the next flight home, his mind racing with a thousand possibilities.

The flight back felt like an eternity. Every bump, every turbulence was a reminder of the fragility of life. As the plane touched down, he rushed to the hospital, his heart pounding in his chest.

The sight of Anvesh lying in a hospital bed was a stark reminder of his own vulnerability. The once vibrant, full of life friend was now pale and still. A wave of guilt washed over Karthik. If only he had stayed in touch, if only he had been there for him.

The doctors explained that Anvesh had been involved in a car accident. The impact had caused severe head injuries. His condition was critical, and the next few days would be crucial.

Karthik sat by Anvesh's bedside, his heart heavy with worry. He blamed himself for not being there for his friend. If he had stayed in touch, perhaps he could have prevented this tragedy.

Ria, who had been informed of the accident, arrived a few days later. Her presence brought a sense of comfort to the bleak hospital room. She sat by Anvesh's bedside, her hand resting gently on his.

Karthik watched them, a pang of jealousy and longing piercing his heart. He had lost Anamika, and now he was risking losing Anvesh. The fear of losing the people he cared about was overwhelming.

Days turned into weeks. Anvesh showed signs of improvement, but the road to recovery was long and arduous. Karthik spent most of his time at the hospital, his world reduced to the sterile environment of the ward.

Ria's visits became a regular occurrence. They would sit by Anvesh's bedside, talking about old times, sharing hopes for the future. Their bond deepened, their friendship a source of strength in the face of adversity.

Karthik found himself drawn to their connection, a bittersweet reminder of the love he had lost. He would often leave the room, seeking solace in the quiet of the hospital corridor. The loneliness was a constant companion, a haunting echo of the pain he had carried for years.

One evening, as he sat alone in the hospital cafeteria, he pulled out his phone. He dialed Anamika's number, his heart pounding in his chest. It had been years since he had heard her voice, and he didn't know what to expect.

The phone rang for a long time before being answered. A stranger's voice informed him that the number was no longer in service. The news hit him like a physical blow. He had lost her, not just as a lover, but as a friend, as a part of his life.

The realization was a bitter pill to swallow. He had clung to the hope of reconnecting, of finding closure. But now, that hope was shattered. He was truly alone.

The loss of contact with Anamika was a wound that refused to heal. Karthik retreated into himself, his world shrinking to the confines of his work and the hospital room where Anvesh lay. He became a ghost, a silent observer of life, his own existence reduced to a monotonous routine.

Months turned into a year. Anvesh, miraculously, recovered, but the experience had left its mark on him. He was a changed man, more cautious, more reserved. Their friendship, while still strong, was tinged with a quiet sadness.

Karthik, under the guise of helping Anvesh recover, had taken over a significant part of his uncle's business. The world of finance and investments was a stark contrast to the realm of medicine, but he found a strange solace in the numbers, the strategies, the calculated risks.

It was a way to channel his energy, to distract himself from the pain. The business grew under his stewardship, a testament to his resilience. Yet, as the empire expanded, so did the loneliness.

He avoided social gatherings, preferring the solitude of his apartment. The fear of encountering someone who knew Anamika was a constant companion. He lived in a self-imposed exile, a prisoner of his own past.

One evening, while going through old files, he stumbled upon a letter from Anamika. It was a letter she had written during their college days, a declaration of her love for him. Reading her words brought a mix of pain and longing.

The letter became a cherished possession, a tangible link to the past. He would often read it, finding solace in her words. It was a bittersweet reminder of a love lost, a love that continued to shape his life.

Karthik was no longer just a businessman; he was a titan of industry. His name echoed in boardrooms and financial circles, a symbol of ambition and success. Yet, amidst the opulence and power, a void persisted.

Anamika was a ghost haunting his memories, a love story unfinished. Every business deal, every strategic move, was a reminder of the life he could have had. Success had become a gilded cage, trapping him in a world of solitude.

His days were filled with meetings, negotiations, and the relentless pursuit of expansion. But as the night fell, the facade of the successful businessman crumbled. The quiet of his penthouse apartment was a stark contrast to the bustling world he inhabited. He would often find himself staring out of the window, lost in thoughts of Anamika.

There were times when he considered reaching out, hoping against hope that she might still be waiting. But the fear of rejection was a formidable opponent. He had built a wall around himself, a fortress of solitude, and breaking it down was a daunting task.

His friends, Anvesh and Ria, had moved on with their lives. They had found love, built families, and carved out successful careers. Their happiness was a constant reminder of what he had lost.

Despite his success, Karthik felt a profound sense of emptiness. He had everything the world deemed desirable, yet he lacked the one thing that truly mattered – love. He was a king of an empty kingdom, a solitary figure in a world of abundance.

The ache of longing was a constant companion. He would often find himself in quiet corners of the world, seeking solace in solitude. The mountains, the beaches, the deserts – they all became his sanctuaries, places where he could escape the relentless demands of his life.

Yet, no matter where he went, the ghost of Anamika followed him. She was a part of him, a love story unfinished, a chapter waiting to be written. And until that chapter found its conclusion, he knew he would be a prisoner of his own past.

The veneer of success began to crack. The man who had conquered the business world was crumbling from within. The occasional business trips, meant to provide a distraction, often turned into solitary confinements, amplifying the echoes of his loneliness.

Breakdown became a frequent visitor. In the quiet of his penthouse, or during the dead of night in a foreign hotel room, the walls would close in. Tears, a foreign entity in the world of business, would stream down his face. Anamika's memory, once a source of pain, now transformed into a haunting obsession.

There were times when the despair was overwhelming. The thought of ending it all, of escaping the prison of his own mind, would creep in. But the memory of her laughter, her spirit, would pull him back from the precipice. She had been his strength, his inspiration, and even in her absence, she continued to be his lifeline.

Work became a refuge, a distraction from the emotional turmoil. He threw himself into projects, deals, negotiations, anything to keep his mind occupied. But the moment there was a lull, the silence would be filled with the echoes of his past.

Hasmitha, his friend, had tried to reach out, to offer support. But Karthik had withdrawn into himself, building a wall around his heart. He feared exposing his vulnerability, afraid of being judged, of being pitied.

The world outside had changed, technology had evolved, and yet, for Karthik, time stood still. He was a man rapped in amber, a prisoner of his own past. The thought of moving on, of finding love again, seemed like a betrayal to Anamika's memory.

He was a successful businessman, admired by many, envied by some. But behind the facade of the powerful CEO, there was a man broken, a heart shattered into pieces. The world knew Karthik the businessman, but only he knew the depth of despair that consumed him.

"Time held no knowledge of his path, nor did the journey reveal its end. Yet, within that passage, he loved with a depth that convinced him she was his ultimate haven. But she abandoned him, leaving him a wanderer lost on an aimless road."

ABOUT THE AUTHOR

Anji Reddy Bapathu is more than just a lecturer; he's a conduit of knowledge, a passionate educator whose vocation transcends the mere transmission of facts. Beyond the academic sphere, Anji Reddy finds solace and expression in the written word. He is a voracious reader, a literary omnivore who devours books across diverse genres, absorbing stories and ideas like a sponge.

For Anji Reddy, writing is not merely a hobby; it's a fundamental need, a way to articulate the intricate tapestry of emotions and observations that resonate within him. He sees writing as a bridge, a means to connect with others on a deeper level, to share the insights gleaned from his experiences and reflections. He possesses a profound understanding of the human condition, and he strives to translate these complexities into evocative prose.

*****